The Kid on Case Mountain

Heaplo

Leaning Rock Press
Gales Ferry, CT

Leaning Rock PressGales Ferry, CT 06335
leaningrockpress@gmail.com
www.leaningrockpress.com

978-1-960596-98-7, Hardcover
978-1-960596-99-4, softcover
978-1-960596-36-9, ebook

Library of Congress Control Number: 2026912995

Publisher's Cataloging-in-Publication Data
(Prepared by Cassidy Cataloguing's PCIP Service)

Names: Plourde, Heather, author.
Title: The kid on Case Mountain / by Heather Plourde.
Description: Gales Ferry, CT : Leaning Rock Press, [2026]
Identifiers: LCCN: 2026912995 | ISBN: 9781960596987 (hardcover) | 9781960596994 (softcover)
Subjects: LCSH: Teenagers. | Coming of age. | Dysfunctional families. | High school students. | Mental health. |
LCGFT: Bildungsromans. | Psychological fiction. | BISAC: FICTION / Coming of Age. | SOCIAL SCIENCE
/ Human Services. | PSYCHOLOGY / Mental Health.
Classification: LCC: PS3616.L68 K54 2026 | DDC: 813/.6--dc23

Printed in the United States of America

Dedication

This is dedicated to the child who found me sitting watching television after school, and looked at me with the kind of honesty only children possess. They told me I was better than that. My children taught me that life was not something to survive quietly, but to live fully, feel every emotion, and reinvent purpose over and over again.

To the friend who told me there is no such thing as "too late." Those words became a lifeline, then a philosophy, then a promise I carried into every new beginning.

To the friend who once said that someday we would have an office with our names on the door. Thank you for seeing a future for me before I could fully see it for myself.

To the town of Manchester — with its beautiful parks, crowded events, hardworking people, and unforgettable characters around every corner. Thank you for teaching me that community is built not through perfection, but through participation, resilience, and heart.

To the teachers, coaches, and parents who volunteer every single time, who stay late, carry the weight quietly, and show up again and again for children and for each other: you are the invisible architecture holding communities together.

To the whimsical women in my community who cheer me on, celebrate loudly, dream freely, and remind me that joy itself is a form of resistance and power.

And to my husband, my true partner — thank you for understanding that love is never ownership, debt, or obligation. It is freedom. It is mutual devotion to building a better life side by side.

Every lesson, every risk, every act of courage carries fingerprints. You reminded me that purpose is not found alone. It is built in the presence of people who call us forward into the fullest version of ourselves.

The Kid on Case Mountain

Heaplo

Author's Note

This story is based on my own experiences working in the mental health field, and is solely my opinion on acute stress disorder (ASD.)

Steven Cookies is portrayed as experiencing ASD and beginning to develop symptoms associated with post-traumatic stress disorder. ASD is a psychological response that can occur shortly after a traumatic event and is characterized by symptoms such as disorientation, emotional numbness, dissociation from reality, difficulty connecting with others, and a persistent sense of danger.

In the story, the narrative structure intentionally reflects these symptoms. The shifts in narrator perspective create a sense of disorientation for the reader, mirroring how individuals with ASD often experience confusion, fragmented memories, and difficulty maintaining stability.

The contrast between different homes and environments also serves a psychological purpose. Rather than offering comfort or safety, each setting feels unstable. This reflects a core symptom of trauma responses: the inability to feel secure even in places that should normally feel safe. For someone experiencing ASD, the world can feel unpredictable and threatening regardless of the surroundings.

Steven's behavior toward others further illustrates dissociation. Instead of moving with people and participating in shared experiences, he moves around them. This narrative choice reflects emotional detachment, a common symptom in trauma responses. Dissociation can cause individuals to feel disconnected from their environment, from other people, and at times even from themselves.

The overall tone of loneliness is therefore intentional. Trauma can create a profound sense of isolation, making it difficult for individuals to emotionally connect or feel present with others. By structuring the story around distance, shifting perspectives, and emotional disconnection, the narrative attempts to place the reader inside Steven's psychological experience.

In this way, the storytelling techniques are not only stylistic choices but also educational representations of how acute stress disorder can affect perception, relationships, and a person's sense of safety in the world.

Prologue

Steven Cookies was a good-looking, charismatic boy with the world at his fingertips. Being Athletic with bright eyes, messy hair, and a relaxed posture made him very likable to everyone, kids and adults alike, in the suburban town of Manchester. His smile could turn heads. He was 15 years old, a sophomore at Manchester High School, an honor student, and never really caused any trouble. Everyone kinda knew him, kinda liked him, never worried about him, and trusted him to always turn up.

You could find Steven jogging after school with the track team on Porter Street, a picturesque street lined with trees and filled with flowers. Although he was involved in everything possible at school, sports, and after-school clubs, no one knew Steven Cookies the way I did. Being retired gives me a lot of free time, and I see more than people think and pride myself on being observant. As a former high school coach, I had to learn to read behavior, and I pay attention to all the things that are not said by everyone. Steven was in trouble, and I was stuck between minding my own business or helping this kid, as a neighbor should.

One day, I realized - We all have to make some choices with our observations, and it's our moral compass that decides on the right thing to do. When your thoughts are statements, that's your conscience. When your mind starts to question, that is anxiety. We are all stuck in the middle of what voice to heed.

I live four houses down from the Case Mountain entrance. I raised a son, worked as a coach, a teacher, and volunteered when I could. Everyone who was 32 years or older around town does this blink thing to me, a weird kinda recognizing respectful wave, acknowledging that I once taught them something at the high school. I don't miss it, teaching that it is. Teaching is a mix of inspiration and violence that makes you addicted to fighting everyone and for your character, all while being blamed for the fall of society and ruled by politicians.

Steven was always quick to give me a smile, a wave, a pat for the dog, or a hand with the lawn. Whenever I could, I hired him to help me and afterwards I would offer him a ride home. He would shrug and say he didn't mind jogging to the other side of Case. "I'll be careful," he would grin. I have offered to call his mom, or have him wait for someone to pick him up while we sit on the sun porch. But with his charming way, he swatted his hand and claimed exercise is what he needed to go to the State meet this year. Whenever I would pressure him to name the house he lived at, he would say, "You know…the house that is kinda beige with the fence…" He hadn't figured out I knew the truth. I knew his real address, his secret, but I didn't know what to do about it.

Early, before 6 am Saturday morning in September, Chunky, my dog, whined at the door, and as I stumbled to the front porch, I found Steven walking out of the Case Mountain trail. I hadn't put my glasses on yet, but it looks like he was fixing himself up. He quickly rinsed his hands in a puddle and put on his sweatshirt. His pace was quick, lively. He looked happy, handsome and well-fed. Yet, the seriousness on his face was hard to look away from, like he could not hide the struggle.

He was about to take off in the opposite direction, and I opened the door, waving. "Hey! What are you doing this early on a Saturday morning- hiking before the sun rises?" Steven gave a smile and a shy glance. He shoved his hands into his track shorts and kinda awkwardly grunted. He quickly ran up to Chunky, happy to run his hands through the thick fur. They both wanted some love this morning, and my heart was warmed by Steven's gentleness.

"I can walk Chunky for you? I don't mind the extra steps," Steven offered quietly. "I even have time this morning. If you want me to mow the lawn for you and give Chunky a good brush?"

I looked at Steven, and my heart just broke. I knew his truth, yet, out of respect for his eagerness to belong, be useful, I couldn't bring myself to embarrass him. He had such an air to him that made me instantly root for him. Although his clothes were not the cleanest, he did seem fed and happy. I always offered him odd jobs, even though I didn't need much help. I never minded the company, and Abby, my wife, always had a stash of doughnuts in case Steven ran by. As I retired from coaching four years ago, and enjoyed putzing around the house, it was a weird sense of loneliness. The only hobbies for my age around here are politics, hiking, and grocery shopping. I often think about our honeymoon in Saint Tropez: people of all ages dancing on the beach late into the night, champagne and delicious seafood, tanned, athletic grown-ups just finding new hobbies like sea fishing and skiing now that they are retired. Here, we are all healthcare cash cattle and told to stay home, out of sight, develop type 2 diabetes, arthritis, and cardiac symptoms.

Our kid Joey moved away some time ago, and having someone with energy around was nice. I always did my best to make Steven feel appreciated and put on a big act about how much there is to managing everything. I kinda always thought that if Joey were around, Steven and he would be friends.

"Really? Are you sure you have time? You don't want to go back to sleep and rest on this Saturday morning? I could really use the help walking Chunky… If you got an hour, could you walk her and give a good brush?" I waited and played it up a bit. Chunky loved Steven, and although I enjoyed my walk every morning at 6:30 am, I wanted to help. Find a way to slip a $20 in Steven's hand. That's how I discovered Steven's predicament. In the early sunrise, I had seen him washing his face and armpits in the stream two months ago.

"Chunky?! She is like the best dog! If that would help you?! I think I got the time." Steven's posture changed to upright, and his eyes twinkled. He chatted about cross-country practice not starting until 9 am, and he woke up early. Not all kids that were dealt a bad hand become throwaways.... I put a $20 in his hand as I handed him the leash. "I'll leave her brush on the porch for you, and just come in through the back when you guys are done getting some fresh air."

As they jogged out of sight, one with a tail wagging and the other one chatting away, I got some clean clothes out of my son's old room. Ever since he left for Texas to work, he hasn't had the time to collect his things. This spring, we were going to drive out - but I know he won't mind Steven having some of his old clothes. I put the clothes on the porch with Chunky's brush. I left doughnuts and a tall glass of juice for Steven and water for Chunky in his bowl.

Later, I heard the porch door slide open. He tried so hard to be polite, but scarfed all the food down when I turned my back to him. "Can you stay a little longer and keep her company? You know she will just whine at the door while I trim the walkway. This way she can stay out of trouble." I shrugged and added, "Also, do you mind finishing up the doughnuts? Abby and I are on a diet, and we just can't have them in the house if you know what I mean." After a beautiful September morning trimming, I found the two of them about an hour later, snoozing together in a heap in the sunshine in the corner of my sun porch. Between the smell of fresh cut grass and coffee, accompanied by smiles, I knew the comfort that big old soft dog had given him, and I let them snooze while I drank my second cup. I wasn't sure what to do, but my gut told me something had to be done before Winter.

Later in the morning, Steven walked out of the porch and back up into town to meet his team at the reservoir. I didn't see or hear him. I just knew that he didn't want to overstay, or worse, have me figure it all out. My expectation that he would show up more and more wasn't wrong. Sunday morning, with gray skies brought Steven back out of Case stumbling like he had been up all night. In his track clothes, he looked sadly desperate. That morning, I let it go. I needed the day to think about it.

Chapter 1

Steven's survival skills

School was never a problem for Steven, most kids felt the drudgery of it, the drain of the institutional system. Steven took the day in stride, and did not mind being around students, teachers, and security alike. He went to class, participated, signed up for any opportunities there were. He was neither the star, nor at the bottom of the class and his goal was to stay out of the way and not be noticed.

After school, Steven waved at everyone, told math jokes with the exhausted teachers in the hall, and headed to the locker room. He was able to fit in with the rest of the boys. The locker room wasn't an easy place. There were lots of different types of kids, all shapes and sizes. Your backpack wasn't safe either - so Steven was on high alert as everyone got ready. Some quickly gathered their items and ran out to catch the bus to away games, while others went out to the field to practice. He took his time changing, as he often didn't have any clean clothes with him. He didn't want to draw attention to his need to wash out his socks in the sink at times.

Even though the locker room was a crazy place...Steven just kept his head down, and always stayed to himself there. It was the one place where he didn't smile. He felt on edge - in survival mode. It was a place for him to change his clothes, and a time when no one was looking for him. He used the area as a base camp to use the soap and rinse his clothes if he needed. He'd developed a system to get there first, hide out, and, when the place was the at its fullest, to kinda go undetected. There was also lost-and-found in the corner, and sometimes that was the best option for the next day's clothes. He had two ways of grabbing something out of the lost-and-found corner. The first was to pretend to accidentally trip and stumble, grab whatever, and then laugh it off. The second was to mutter "Oh! That's where this is…" and claim it. He looked for hoodies, clean t-shirts, socks, and sometimes he would notice a water bottle that he could wash and re-use.

Steven started his treasure seeking in May of last year, when he was a freshman. There was treasure in the corner of the lost-and-found. It changed everything and gave him the freedom he now had.

One afternoon, from the other corner of the area, he overheard a few boys talking about their phones and how upset one boy was not to have "upgraded" since middle school. The boy in his Adidas outfit and expensive sneakers bragged about setting the phone to factory settings and claiming it was lost or stolen in the locker room. The kids then cracked the bottom of the screen as it was tossed to the bottom of the pile. Steven stood there frozen - almost paralyzed with the thought of having a phone. It would give him access to his homework and so many other important things. The struggle he was having with basic necessities and being able to access sign-ups, learning how to buy bus passes, ordering food - this would be a game-changer. He had been relying only on his school-issued Chromebook, which had limitations.

Once the coast was clear, Steven walked casually near the pile of clothes that were left in a dirty heap from the week. As the locker room started to empty, and boys were in their small groups and cliques, Steven dodged into the bin and wrapped his fingers around this priceless find. Even with a cracked screen, this gave him so much more independence than he had planned on. He noticed the phone's battery was low. He had to figure out how to charge the phone and where he could plug it in. He would need to look for a phone case and cord in other lost-and-found bins, and it would be his from now on. With wi-fi and his Apple ID, he would be able to sign up for more opportunities and never struggle with the monsters again.

In the bin was another score, a Nike t-shirt with ketchup on it. He could scrub the stain, and it would feel good to have the soft cotton after his jog. Steven snatched both the shirt and phone and stuffed them in his bag as he stealthily walked out of there.

Between the phone, shirt, and free lunch, that was the day Steven planned his new life at the age of 14.

He had twenty minutes before needing to be on the field, so he swiftly walked back into the school and stopped to ask Mr. Gus, a long-time security guard, if anyone had handed in a phone charger. Mr. Gus silently shook his head "no," but pointed to the main office sign. Steven darted to the main office and saw a lost-and-found bin there as well. He had not known about this bin until today. With all his manners, he asked the secretary if he could look for a phone charger, and she gave a silent "yes." There he found a tattered cord, a sticky plug, and a scratched phone case. In one hour, everything came together - and he was free.

After track, sitting in the corner of the McDonald's, 2 miles away from the high school, sweaty from the long-distance run earlier with the team, he put it all together and hoped, like he never had before, that everything worked. After he found a used soda cup, swished water around it to rinse it out, and refilled it with soda, it was time to put all the phone items to the test. Once the cord, case, and phone were all together, it felt like it was truly his, and he wrote his name - Steven Cookies- on it. He began charging the phone because the phone screen showed 10%. He joined the free Wi-Fi…and success! While he sat there, he set up his first email account, added the monster's account, and loaded apps for school, real estate, and gas station rewards for the snacks. Now he was on his own.

He finished his homework, and as the long day came to an end, washed up in the restaurant bathroom, and walked slowly to his secret place, feeling content. As he neared the millwork intersection, he thought he saw Him, the Monster, and shivers ran down his spine - Did He see him back? Was it a silver truck or dark grey? Steven convinced himself it was all his imagination, that no one was following or recognized him. In Steven's secret world, there were worse things than neglect. There were monsters. They drove a truck, stole medicine, and abused him for their own use. Tonight, he would not return to that place. He would find a way to live with the dignity he so wanted.

Chapter 2

The Monsters

Steven Cookies hated the amount of junk food he had to eat; he dreamed of nice big salads with lots of fresh green colorful vegetables, homemade salad dressings, and a beautiful expensive steak like you see in movies. Instead, he really lived off of whatever he could get his hands on while walking from place to place or from the school cafeteria. He went to Cumberland Farms often and would call it his favorite restaurant. Everyone there was like his extended family - Sal, Evie, and Evan all helped him and always had something special waiting for him, whether it was a free bag of chips or a Slushie. There, his $20 could last a week. There were three bananas for a dollar or a large chocolate chip cookie. He'd have to sacrifice this time, though, because he needed $18 for his museum field trip with his Cultural Club.

In the middle of Spanish class, where he quietly worked on his project so he didn't have to worry about finding ways to study and complete it after school, the phone in the classroom rang, and everyone shhh'd out of curiosity. "You want Steven?" - "Steven who?" - "No, I only have Steven Cookies in my room…." Ms. Rodriquez, a tired, middle-age single parent/teacher, who ran the after-school group called "Espanol," huffed. Steven's heart was in his throat as everyone turned and stared at him.

"Steven Conski?" My teacher craned her weary head around and looked at me. "Is that your name? Steven Conski?"

I shrugged, as I felt everyone side-eye me. In third grade, I was terrorized and teased constantly by two boys. They called me Steven Cookies because I was a bit chubby, never had sneakers that fit, and couldn't run. Finally, after a year of being tortured, pushed, and punched when the teachers weren't looking, I stood my ground. One boy - we will call him bully #1 - tried to trip me, and instead, I stomped on his kneecap as hard as I could, and then whispered, "You were outsmarted by Steven Cookies." From that moment on, as a nine-year-old, I decided Steven Conski was a small, chubby kid who was bullied, was mistreated, and shown no respect. I wanted to blur that boy into oblivion, never to be associated with Conski again. But! Steven Cookies was a smart, strong boy who would always try to find a way and do the right thing.

When starting middle school, during the first day of orientation, I went to the office and explained to the secretary that there was a glitch. Steven Cookies was my real name. She was 100 years old, and not very interested. She looked me up and down and changed it - Just like that! Someone had listened and fixed it for me. It was an amazing feeling because my birth name gave me goosebumps! I would much rather be re-named by my nemesis than my monsters.

"Can you go to the office?" Ms. Rodriquez asked. I nodded and left, imagining myself drifting out like a ghost. Very faintly, everyone could see me, but I know everyone felt me, the sour, sweaty nerves with a tinge of lost self-worth. I got up and packed my things. I already knew there was going to be a monster waiting for me. It was going to feel like I was drowning, with my chest gasping for air in shallow breaths. I wanted to run and not go - but I knew it was better to face my monsters than run from them. Running just made the chase more dramatic, and like a dying mouse to a cat, more interesting.

I walked down the empty hallway. The high school was full of over one-thousand students and maybe five hundred teachers and staff, yet the hallway felt like an abandoned space station. There was no one to smile and wave at me, no one to distract me from what was in the office. I was more alone in those three minutes than all the past three weeks since school started back.

With my head down, I fist bumped the guard in front of the office and slowly entered through the heavy door. My mother was waiting in the office, smiling and chatting with the same secretary who never spoke to me. Like they were both normal, like my life was normal. Like this was all normal. Yet when my mother greeted me, she acted like I was an issue she had to take care of on the way to the nail salon and grocery store. She was dressed in regular clothes, and she looked so everyday. It was easy for her to fit into a world of humans. No one knowing she was a monster. The embarrassment and harassment I was going to hear from her learning that I had changed my name would be severe. But why did she come here? I hadn't seen her in eleven days and 4.2 hours.

We locked eyes right there as I shuffled through the door. She squinted just enough for me to catch, and no one else. She looked around the office as if she had dropped something and casually thanked the staff. To be fair, I was beyond hope that I would make it back here, with teachers, homework, other bullies, and the track team. I was never sure if these were my last moments or not. My ears stopped working, and there was a faint throb inside my throat. My thoughts raced. As my mother collected herself and issued thanks and praise to the security guards, she reached her arms towards me to rest on my shoulders. I dodged and walked ahead by three paces without looking up.

In American History, we had read about being captured by people from ICE, or in WWII being caught behind enemy lines. I felt like I was the only person in the room who understood that emotion of being captured with no hope of returning, the claustrophobia of not knowing how much power would be asserted onto you as a person. Would it be mental? Physical? Both? Would I be ok? Would I have a choice?

Without a greeting to me directly, she storms ahead toward the car. I just understand that it is my directive to follow. With head down, no eye contact, and no words, I obediently got into the dark blue SUV. The one that smelled like moldy cigarettes and deodorant. I could not let any words out of my throat. I only opened the passenger side door, put my seat belt on, and waited. Besides the car smelling like old cleaning fluid, old perfume, bad car fresheners, and dirty underpants, there are small empty nippers rolling around, peeking out from underneath the seat with every stop at every red light. They bounce off my worn sneaker heel.

As much as I cannot speak, my mother also sits withdrawn and in silence. I have no idea if it is chemical, emotional, or the faint ticking of her temper. Finally, as we drive further from the high school, further from my comfort zone, further from the places I know how to "get by" and "fit in," her voice cracks, "Well - I didn't realize our name is not good enough for you. It took me all morning to find you. Who knew you would be at school this whole time? With the way you are, thinking you're better than us, I thought you had run away completely."

I sit in silence with no response, slowly shrinking into my own abyss. I want to demand answers. "Where are we going! Why are you here now! What is going to happen to me!" Yet, instead of controlling my voice and speaking, the words form into tears, and they will not stop rolling down my face. I quickly try to hide them, but the tears are coming too fast, and out of nowhere, I gulp air to try to.....I don't know what to do.

We pulled into a medical office that I vaguely remember. A scene enters my forehead, and I feel like I have been smacked with the memory. Screaming, threatening, lying, and being dragged by the shirt when I refused to enter years ago. I did not know what a dentist was. I think I was four years old. The young girl who set me in the chair gave me "the look" most adults give me. Their chin down, and eyes up with their head cocked slightly to one side. I noticed I get this look more than anyone else in the room, anywhere when I was with my mother. She put a bib on me, and cartoons on a screen. Once she feverishly set up the scene, she darted out, bringing back into the area a "Dad-like" man of some sort. No one told me what to do. I could hear my mother talking, and pretending like she was once again normal. I envisioned her earlier putting on her "mom suit" while she put on some makeup. I knew then there was a monster behind the lipstick.

I was horrified and scared. I couldn't stop shaking and crying. I tried so hard to comply with the dentist telling me to be still and open my mouth. I was even more scared when I saw him recoil once I opened wide. I picked up the word "rot" and that my teeth wouldn't last much longer. I don't remember much else from the white coat man, but I do remember the sweet girl giving me extra bags of toothbrushes, and attempting to show me what they were and how to use them. From there, I remember being pushed down the stairs after leaving the office, falling down the flight and hurting my elbow, the same elbow my monster wrenched and lifted me off the ground with, shoving me through the exit. I cried, and not knowing how to make my legs work, I stumbled again, this time taking down the two of us. I woke up at some point after not knowing if I had dreamt it all.

Now the building is in front of me again, and I am no longer 4-year-old Steven Conski. I am Steven Cookies, a capable person who can overcome this nightmare, and I will learn and pay attention. I will take business cards and speak up if I am alone or if I can.

Mother looks at me and tries to do the "loving look." Her voice is hard to concentrate on, but she tries. "Steven, we are in big trouble. You have to go to the dentist, and I hope this is quick because we have a visitor at four o'clock. There was a complaint that you are on the track team and after school activities, with no medical forms. Did you use fake forms, Steven?" I paused, kept my eyes down. "Well!," She continued, "thanks to that, DCF (Department of Children and Families) has been called on me and your father." I swallowed. The idea of seeing my father knowing I caused him to interact with me or anything regarding me, was enough to cool a lava lamp.

"S - s -s- so," I stammered. "So what happens now? Am I going to jail?" What if my father, mother, and I all go to jail? Would I share a cell with my father? Clearly my mother would be sent to a women's prison. I can't control my anxiety. The ideas are coming too fast.

"Well, we have to go to the dentist, and then you will come home! And! You will do as I say." She sounded so authoritative yet out of control, a wild card. I exited the car and let my mind drift. Thoughts that entered and floated away were: run, hide in the bathroom when she wasn't looking, beg for forgiveness to a judge for lying on my medical form, tell the truth. Thoughts and schemes start to weigh less and take up less space in my mind as I walk. I am aware that my legs have gone numb as I climb the stairs that lead to the dentist.

I comply. I want to be in school, I want to feel the sweet breeze of Porter Street while I run with a group that all have the same goal. I want to feel the thick fur of Chunky and her cute embrace when I squat down to say hello. I don't want to do as I'm told now, I don't want to be with monsters. I let all my will go, and just comply.

Chapter 3

Home

With a crisp report from the dentist, that I have one cavity that needs to be filled and could use braces, but it's not necessary, we drive home. The paper was clasped and put into a purse that only came out when she had to carry things for me. I will never see those records, or probably that dentist ever again. We drove through town in silence. Yet all of our mixed emotions are screaming with tension between us. It felt like electricity, and all we needed was a spark. I sat motionless. I can feel her hurt, a sense of confusion on how to handle me, anger, betrayal. I wonder what she feels for me? Surely that maternal, unconditional love is a fairy tale.

We pull into the driveway of my captors. I envision this place like a dark castle, full of mysterious secrets, but it really was just a nice home on the west side of town. I go to open the door of the car with heavy legs, but Mother grabs my arm and looks at me with wild eyes. "You go straight upstairs, shower, and put on clean clothes! And hurry - it's almost 4 o'clock." I nod, take a deep breath, and try to go numb again, which would be preferred over the fear. In order to face that feeling, there are different stages - like descending an imaginary staircase. First, your ears stop working, and instead, your blood pressure increases only in the ears. Your lungs deflate and cannot coordinate. My legs become fleshy anchors made of jello-like flab, that takes a huge amount of effort to synchronize in any direction. My eyes dart, blinking, screaming thoughts. Run! Hide! Stand up for yourself! Say no! Comply! Say yes. It will be ok. Your mother loves you. She must love you in some way. It's going to be ok. You can get through this. Maybe this time it will be ok. You want them to love you…. and the thinking will not slow down.

***

Steven opens the front door, as it was never locked. He wouldn't know how to lock it if he wanted to. The deadbolt had been taken apart years ago, and although the metal box is still on the door frame, the remnants of that tough moment in the middle of the night show on the inside frame. Entering the house, the smell hits you first. It's not a bad smell, just that of depression, leftovers rotting in the trash, bad perfume, old potpourri, and a bit of alcohol. The autopilot takes over, and before he realizes it, Steven is in the shower and for the first time in a long time, it feels nice to be home. It almost lulls him into forgetting all the dark moments and remembering the good that happened here within the walls. The holidays, when they were together in peace. The hot water and fresh shampoo'd hair is exactly what he needed.

After a few minutes of getting lost in the bubbly soap, he remembered there was a visitor coming. Is it the police who will take him away? He knew falsifying his school record was wrong, but he had no choice in August. Two years ago, Steven's mother had shared her email and password with him so that he could sign in for her while she rested on the couch. He never forgot it and has been using her email to get him into school. With a towel around his waist, he goes into his room, shuts and locks the door, and leans into the wall. Although he was here eleven days ago, he didn't remember the dust an inch thick on everything. The way the sun came in through the filmy window put a weird yellow light on the furniture. Making the room feel like his past.

Everything from eighth grade was there: the soccer ribbon, robotics buttons, and pictures of his "friends" who do not acknowledge him anymore. The clothes, furniture, and bed are three sizes too small. The room was a coffin full of his younger life, weird dress outfits from toddlerhood and shoes that never fit. He grabbed some clothes, and with great pleasure, fresh underwear. As he looked for his backpack to stuff extra clothes, panic set in. The cardinal rule in the locker room was to never leave your stuff unattended, and here his backpack was nowhere to be found. What if Mother takes it, all the things he would lose, cell phone, Chromebook, deodorant? All the things he cannot replace. His backpack was left in the car.

Steven hurries downstairs. He is startled to find a young, pretty girl with a canvas messenger bag across her chest and a large badge on a red string around her neck standing at the end of the stairs waiting. The badge had big letters D.C.F.

Shocked, he doesn't know what to say or expect. They don't get visitors, only intruders. His mother begins talking rapidly, making claims that Steven knows aren't true. She insists that he's never been hit, that they encourage and help him. As she speaks, she mentions that his father will be home soon—something that makes the hairs on Steven's neck stand up.

The worker stands there nodding, shifting from one foot to the other, with glazed eyes. Mother never let her past the front area. The woman wears a half-smile and looks half-annoyed, half-robotic. Her voice was sweet and soft, and she interrupts the rambling of my nervous mother. "Can I speak to Steven now?" Mother starts to slow down her trail of explanations, and reluctantly agrees by nodding her head. I couldn't tell if she was shaking from nerves or annoyance. But she stepped down the hall a bit, stumbling for a half step towards the kitchen. I was surprised someone so forceful could be unnerved by a sweet, pretty young lady. This made Steven aware of who had power in the moment and who did not.

Steven, wearing clothes a size too small, slowly moves into the living room hugging, the wall and making his way to the couch. He notices his backpack lying by the door and cannot avert his eyes from anything else. The woman takes it upon herself to follow him and sit in the chair with my father's imprint in the bottom cushion. She puts her bag down, takes out a printed piece of paper, and flips through a double-sided report. He knows better than to say anything, so he waits to answer. He knows his mother is nearby waiting to interject if needed.

Steven quietly nods and shakes his head to every question. As the story is pieced together in his head, he loses any memory of the questions. After blanking on the couch, his head snaps up when his mother sits down next to him.

"Steven, you should have put on clothes that fit." she giggles". His eyes watered, and his throat gulped quietly. He is convinced his mother wouldn't know what size to buy him.

Steven thinks about the small bag of clothes he keeps at his campsite and mentally notes that he only has one day's worth of clean clothes left. He will have socks, but nothing else here will do. He can only hear his own heartbeat loudly in his ears, as if there aren't any other sounds on earth.

When the DCF worker leaves, Mother's tone shifts. She begins slapping him, yelling that the school called DCF because of him. Steven grabs his backpack, but she fights him for it, shouting that he doesn't deserve anything. The bag rips as he wrestles it away. Tears well up as he breaks free, sprinting for the door—only to run straight into his father.

His father grabs his shoulder hard, but Steven wriggles free and bolts down the street. He grips the torn bag and contents as if his life depended on it. Eventually, he makes it back to his campsite—his only safe place. While on the run, he noticed Coach and the dog Chunky staring. With his head down he makes sure there was no eye contact, and no one in the busy trails saw where he went.

Chapter 4

Campsite discovered

Steven had built a strange kind of order into his campsite, a system that made sense only to him. At the center of it all was a large fake boulder he'd stolen one sleepless night from a house a mile away. The guilt of taking it never really left him. He told himself he'd return it someday.

The house he'd taken it from had a rock garden, serene and deliberate, almost meditative, though if you looked from the right angle, it resembled something alien, like a crop circle carved in stone. The boulder itself was hollow, a shell of light foam meant to disguise the old well in the yard. Now it sat deep in Case Mountain, hiding Steven's supplies.

Through the past year, he'd moved his camp several times, each time more carefully than before. Soon it would be time to move again. When he used the boulder, he disguised it with moss, logs, and stones, sometimes obsessing over its camouflage until it looked more like an art project than a hiding place. Other days, no matter how much he covered it, he couldn't shake the feeling that it was standing out, that he was exposed.

Under the fake boulder, Steven kept his personal things. Inside a plastic bag sat another dead cell phone, service long disconnected. He couldn't bring himself to throw it away. His mother had given it to him, and he feared she might someday accuse him of losing it. Next to it was a small pocket knife from a Cape Cod gift shop, a souvenir his grandfather had bought him when he was six. There was also a faded coin purse stamped Educator.

He kept a few pairs of sweatpants, shorts, and t-shirts, all scavenged from lost-and-found boxes at the school and a church two miles away. His sneakers were worn thin, but he tried to keep them clean and dry. Once, he'd found a few mismatched pairs in a recycling bin and grabbed what he could.

His mother once let it slip that his grandparents were sick — one with cancer, the other with dementia. They never visited again. But that long weekend in their house left him with something lasting: a spark. Their love was proof that he could be loved.

He had a small green tent, a green tarp that had blown off a truck on the interstate, and a pair of winter sweatpants he used as a sleeping bag. He charged his phone at the library on weekends, at school during the week, and sometimes at Dunkin' Donuts or McDonald's if the weather and walking suited him. The main issue was Wi-Fi on the mountain.

One neighbor near Case Mountain, on the north side, had two large dogs. Steven would hear them being called early in the morning if he was camped under the big rock wall. His tent fit almost perfectly beneath it, hidden from view on the path above. He tried guessing the neighbor's Wi-Fi password one day using the dogs' names, and voilà! It turned out to be their names with a "2."

Making my campsite was a process, and I cannot say for how long I planned or thought about it. Over time, I found myself more and more in the woods. By the first few days of school starting, I was sore all over. My legs burned, my back ached, and the bug bites made it impossible to think straight, and dreaded poison ivy was bubbling up on my arms and hands. Now, with everything he owned and all the fear in the world, his boulder was all he wanted to see.

Steven stopped and checked out the backpack. Although it was torn, he could still make it work. Finding a lost backpack might be hard, but it was on his mental list. Out of nowhere, tears fell from his eyes, and the sweet shampoo smell made it impossible not to feel all his senses. He wasn't sure if it was knowing he was safe on Case Mountain, if he knew this wasn't safe at all, or if the tears were for grieving all he knew as a child. But the sound of children yelling and playing near his boulder alerted him.

Steven slowly walked up to the rock cropping to find some kids running and climbing on the boulders. His fake rock was off to the side, kind of away from the rock ledges, but it still must have looked tempting to one of the boys. Steven immediately quickened his pace to get closer to his rock when one of the boys ran past him and jumped on the fake boulder. Steven dropped the backpack and gulped. The boys instantly knew the rock was different, and Steven started running towards him. The boy climbed down and felt the fake stone. Steven gathered his voice to yell "stop", and then they all heard "Get over here!" The infamous mom voice echoing made everyone in the vicinity stop and look around.

The mother called her children back, and reluctantly they complied. The boy knocked past Steven, but glancing over his shoulder at the strange find. This made Steven want to run over there and check everything out. He hadn't thought about whether people would climb on his boulder when he wasn't there. He had assumed it was disguised. This was another problem that needed a solution.

Case Mountain is actually a park in Manchester, Connecticut, with a majestic waterfall and lots of rock outcroppings from mining years and years ago. With a patch of forest and viewpoints, it made a popular hiking spot in eastern Connecticut. For Steven, it was his new home. With the fear that someone else would find his boulder, Steven made the decision to wait for the sun to set. That's when the mountain quieted down and a better time for him to relocate. Not that teenagers didn't stumble in, or dog walkers didn't come through. But mostly after the sun went down, the mountain was just for Steven.

Once the night grew still, Steven started the laborious trek of packing up everything to find a new spot. It would have to be near other rocks, so he could hide his stuff and blend in with the landscape. The walk wasn't far, but between nerves about being found, the energy he'd expended earlier, and all his anxiety, Steven struggled. Admittedly, this was one of the worst days, and in a strange optimism, tomorrow would have to be better.

Steven looked for a good site to settle where the ground level enough. This was not an easy task either. There wasn't much time for him to set up the tent and get comfortable. So he just kinda collapsed, and let whatever sleep happen. There would be monsters in his dreams this night, he was sure, and Steven was not ready for another battle. Anxiety of not knowing how this story would end was almost too much to bear.

Chapter 5

Bad day

Steven woke up completely covered in morning mist, and everything had a limp, wet feel. September on Case Mountain was full of gnats, poison ivy, and poison oak due to the change of season. The crisp air was cold and wet through the night, and Steven would have to find a way or a place that was dry.

As he stretched, tried to make sense of everything, and fix all his problems while the sun rose, he felt defeated. His Chromebook was not charged for school, he had a headache, and nothing was clean or dry. It would be a difficult walk to Manchester High being completely wet.

First period pre-algebra sucked. Everything went wrong. The cord to charge his Chromebook wasn't working, and it had a $20 replacement fee to get a new one. The teacher had no patience for anyone. He could not concentrate on anything, just the dull stabbing pain in his temple and stiff neck from sleeping on the ground.

Steven's second class was art, and every other student there had a Paraeducator to help them- or so it seemed. Normally, Steven kept his head down, studied, and made very little fuss. But when another student grabbed his journal and scribbled on it, he lost it. He lunged at the student and ripped it out of his hands, making it seem like a fight was about to break out. That did not end well.

During lunch, the main dish was spaghetti, which is the least appetizing lunch item they served. It consisted of watered-down sauce that tasted like ketchup on a doughy, soggy bird's nest. He ate it anyway. He'd eat whatever food he could get. He hadn't had breakfast due to being late in the morning. The day dragged on, nothing went well, no one was happy, everyone was miserable, especially Steven.

During study hall, he went to the nurse's office to get some aspirin and have her look at the itchy, painful rash on his arms. He wasn't sure if it was a bug bite, acne, or something worse. She, with very little interest, rubbed some cortisone and left it at that. They both ignored his growling stomach with a shrug.

Steven's day had gone from bad to worse. His back ached from sleeping wrong and carrying everything he owned, the bug bites on his arms burned and itched beneath his shirt, even though the nurse rubbed medicine on them. He was exhausted, tired, and fed up with everything: the noise at school, the looks, the endless small talk. By the end of the afternoon, after the rest of his classes, he just needed to find peace and quiet.

He started walking aimlessly through the hallways, worried about the rain forecast for that night. As he headed towards the doors, ready to skip cross-country he noticed the cubby corner closet was open. This was a food pantry of sorts for students who could not get food. Steven turned on his charm and wandered over. "I can help you stock some shelves?" he said charmingly.

The volunteer from the women's league smiled and gave him the "awww" look. "I don't need much help today, but you are such a good boy to offer." The staff member smiled sweetly and turned away.

Gathering courage and humility Steven gulped out, "Can I have some food to take home? Maybe some crackers and peanut butter.

"You need to hand in a form that states your family income. Do you qualify for free lunch?" as she grabbed a clipboard with a few pages of names on a list.

Steven wasn't sure, so he disguised his desperation with a shrug.

"This food is for the needy," she replied, shrugged, frowned, and continued with her day. So, with his stomach growling, he continued on with his day. It wasn't anything unusual. He would figure something out later. He always did.

Along the trail that crossed the ridge of Case Mountain, his shoes scuffed over the roots and loose gravel until the path sloped down toward the far side, the part where hardly anyone went. He sat down trying to make sense of his decisions, of everyone else's decisions. Why is the world the way it was?

That's when the blaring horn from a red SUV startled everything. An older woman in her car was head-to-head with a white sedan. The old road on Case is a one-lane. One car goes, then the next side. That is how most people in the neighborhood handle it. Instead, today, the two women became adversaries: obscenities, horns, shouting, insults, refusal to move. Both monsters felt they should dominate, that the road was only for them, their needs, their consumption. Monsters that will go home and be ungrateful, never learn to love, never gain respect of the world around them, only their self-petrified pity. Steven was disgusted and slowly walked to camp, the sick sounds of monsters behind him.

The air was heavy with late-summer humidity, thick with the smell of pine and dirt as he wound his way to the campsite. It was still too early to get things out from his rock. He always waited until the last moments of sunset. He was going to wait it out, worried that someone else would find his boulder. Leery and ready to give up, he saw something curious while sitting on a log next to the hidden boulder. The family that lived behind Case Mountain had a for sale sign in the yard. He realized they had finally moved to Florida, like a few months ago, when the owner told him he was ready to retire and Steven had stopped to greet him.

I used to shovel their driveway in the winter, and every time they would curse the weather and tell me how they are going to be winter birds soon. The windows were all blacked out, yet the house had a warm, welcoming look, like everyone who lived there was happy. As I stood on the hill overlooking the house, thunder cracked over my head, and my heart jumped almost out of my body, making my knees buckle.

What should I do? How can I stay out here? Maybe if I stay near the garage of the empty house it would be safer. I wandered into the yard, worried about cameras. The night was very dark, and I didn't have anywhere else to turn. I was planning on hiding next to the house instead of using my tent. Everything was still wet, and the night was too dark to sort it out. Lost and panicked, I saw the window in the garage was open, and, out of curiosity, and just out of curiosity I peeked in. I couldn't help it. I don't want to overstep, impose, or break laws, but somehow I couldn't keep the pull of being in shelter out of my chest. Just sitting in a dry garage, even for a few hours, would be such a relief. As I stood there longing to be inside, thunder cracked again, and I leaped through the window so fast I don't know how I even made it. I shouldn't. I knew that. But I am so tired, the kind of tired that feels like it sits in your bones.

I stood there for a long time, listening. Nothing. Not even a car passing by. The whole neighborhood was still, and it was like the world knew the storm was about to come. Inside smelled like dust and soap. I didn't dare turn on the lights, but when I flipped a switch just to check, the power still worked. I turned it right back off, afraid someone would see me through the windows, and I would be arrested or something worse, sent to live with other monsters. It didn't feel right to be there, but it somehow felt so good at the same time.

The door to the house was unlocked, and I just needed a place for a bit, until the rain stopped. What if I was found there, what would happen to me? As I contemplated right from wrong, being inside a home was magical. I knew the family had said every time I passed them, to stop by if I needed something. Although what

I needed would never be found in an empty house, I knew I was welcome at this moment. The whole place, although half empty, still felt like the walls retained positive family energy.

The floors creaked softly beneath my shoes, worn by a busy family. Because I didn't dare to touch anything, I had to feel my way through the dark with my arms outstretched. The stabbing thoughts of what would happen if I was found, were hard to control. So I kinda took smaller steps, felt my way around, and moved carefully, guided by the thin beam from my phone. I went to the laundry room next to the garage and found some soap and cleaning supplies left. I quickly took my outer clothes off and threw them and what I had in my backpack in without thinking. Survival was all I felt. Now that I was down to my boxers and t-shirt, I realized I hadn't thought this through.

Not sure what to do, knowing I had to wait at least 45 minutes for my clothes, I went back to the garage to sit still. The storm was heavy, and I didn't mean to cause any trouble or take advantage of their home. As I sat down on a bucket, I accidentally spilled a plastic tub of oil. Quickly making the bucket upright, oil splashed onto my leg and arms, and once again I was in a mess I had created.

How do I always make everything worse? Just then, the storm cracked outside, and the rain was hitting the roof so hard that it felt like I was in space, not in Manchester, Connecticut. With my heart racing, I decided to go inside and try to clean up. If I leave without a trace, it will be ok. I will fix this. I know the dad. I am grateful I had helped him that winter to shovel when his back was hurt. I knew he wasn't a monster.

I carefully wandered through the kitchen, and although my stomach ached, and my chest was tight with fear, I really needed to get the oil off me, my clothes dry, and go home… to my boulder. The house was large, and just when I was deciding which way to go and what to look for, the lighting cracked, illuminating the whole place. Although it was for only half a second, it showed me so much. This was a happy house, with soft colors and remnants of card games with laughter, but a shiver of fear still went down my spine.

I climbed the stairs and found the bathroom with a linen closet. Picturing a shower in the sparkling bathroom made me wary that I would get caught, or not be able to clean the shower up. So instead, I filled the tub with hot water, found some soap, and climbed in. The hot water stung at first, but then it felt like heaven. The water turned murky brown fast, and I didn't want to get out. The rain was hitting hard, the washing machine whirled, and I was warm and safe. If I could freeze time…

In my sleepy daze, I heard an alarm go off, startling me. As quietly as I could, I drained the tub, dried off, and dashed into the nearest bedroom to make sure it wasn't something I'd set off. Realizing the alarm wasn't anything to be scared of, but that my clothes were washed, I had to run and put them in the dryer. I was about to go downstairs when I realized I was still naked. Trying to work out if I should borrow something to wear, I made a mental note to bring everything back and wandered into a bedroom at the end of the hall to search for clothes. The "borrowing' was something I would make right someday, and my list grew daily, and I will never forget the people on it.

The walls in the back room were bare now, but a faint outline showed where posters once hung. The bed had clean sheets, soft and smelling of laundry soap. I couldn't possibly lie down. I didn't deserve it. I had made a mess in the garage and used their stuff without permission. But touching the bed for a few seconds made me want to weep. This was not something I should use. I didn't deserve it after being so needy and coming in here.

I opened the dresser drawers and found underwear and socks in the top drawer, a t-shirt and sweatshirt that said "Boston" in the middle drawer, and some sweatpants that were way too big in the last drawer. I looked around the room to make sure I left no trace, when I saw something so precious, I couldn't believe it: sneakers, royal blue running sneakers that were clean and dry. If I take these, I will have to work off the cost with the family.

Maybe send them a letter and let them know. Would they call the Police? Or report me? Or should I just fess up to being a terrible person? After calming down, l have decided to offer to work off the cost by shoveling and yard work. The sneakers were still sitting on top of the box - and… fit so well, it was like they were left just for me. I felt the love from the mom who'd bought these for her son to run in. I felt guilty taking that from him, the boy who must have grown up here, but I promised myself not to take the gift for granted.

As the thunder and lightning cracked right over the house, I wiped up the entire bathroom, hung the towel on the rack, and climbed down the stairs carefully to not make any other messes. I did not want to disturb the house or the family anymore. It was important to me not to take the things this night has given me for granted: safety, comfort, protection, warmth. I knew I had to leave everything in order to get the family to understand how hard this night was.

I put my clothes in the dryer. The rain and wind were still strong. I would have to wait it out. I wandered into the living room and felt my way around. While waiting for my clothes to dry, I sat down on the floor against the couch to ensure no on from the road would see me inside the house through the large picture window.

Sleep hit hard, deep, and dreamless.

When he woke, the moon was high. His heart pounded. He didn't know where he was at first. Then it hit him. He collapsed on the fluffy living room carpet huddled against the couch, and needed to leave. What if someone had seen a light? What if there was a camera? What if the realtor came by? A couple of deep breaths pushed the panic down, and Steven realized it was 2 am. Not just the house was silent, it felt like the town was holding its breath, and it was only his heart in his ears that made any noise.

He sat there for an immeasurable amount of time, frozen, listening to the faintest hum of the refrigerator and the faint creaks of the house settling. Shame rolled over him, not for being there, but for how good the carpet had felt, how clean and happy everything seemed. It was hard to accept that there are ways to live in a house that is not angry and sad.

He got up quietly and roamed through the kitchen cabinets. His stomach ached so badly. He would add whatever he ate to the tally he mentally calculated. He found a packet of ramen noodles in a drawer and a couple of ketchup packets in the fridge. He cooked the noodles in the microwave, stopping the timer before it beeps, not wanting to break the silence. He ate. His hunger pains causing stomach cramps in the dark room as he stared at himself in the faint glow of the microwave clock. He did not like what he saw.

Afterward, he cleaned everything, wiped the counters, folded the towel he'd used, double checked to make sure the tub was spotless, and any evidence of him was gone. Taking two garbage bags, he double-bagged all of his belongings because he knew everything at his campsite would be wet from such a big storm. Then he lay on the floor in the garage with a blanket that was left behind, too restless to sleep. He watched the window for the first trace of dawn.

When the light finally crept in, he slipped out the same way he'd come, careful not to leave a mark. The air outside was cool, and for a moment, he just stood there, breathing it in. He needed to check on the campsite, but for a moment, pretending that he was still safe this morning was a game he liked to play.

Steven walked to school.

Chapter 6

Hunger Pains

Saturday morning felt different. There was an early-morning cross-country meet, but on the other side of town, and Steven had no way of getting there. It almost felt like the world was spinning and leaving him behind. Besides the team meeting 7 miles away, Steven had no money or way to find food today. Yesterday, although he felt productive after school and had cleaned and dried all his clothes, everything was starting to catch up with a headache and chills. Knowing his team and where he could hide in the fabric of society was out of reach, made him depressed. He longed to be with the others kids his age, and around the moms who brought cookies and doughnuts. Instead, he woke up and had to hide the truth and live in silence.

I realized then, that I would have to give myself structure to get through the long weekend. Although I couldn't be at Wickham Park representing the school, I could make sure my laundry was washed. I went for a run anyway and found a way to make money and eat. There were other homeless people in the area, but thankfully, they kept their distance, the way I would from them, too. I am not homeless, I am in transition.

Grabbing one of the extra trash bags from Monday night, I started looking for cans and bottles. I also picked up random trash, because the thought that I was living in a dump zone for toddler snack packs and loose mittens, took away the sense of pride from being free. After a while, I had a trash bag full of cans to return, and proudly went off to Highland Park Grocer to collect my fare. After returning the cans, I had $3.25! And the thought of eating something made me smile.

In a small community grocery store, nothing is cheap, and that also made Steven nervous. He craved healthy foods and eating until he was so full he could burst. Carefully, he walked the aisles and produce section, trying to figure out the biggest meal he could get with him money. He picked up a fist-sized apple and placed it in his basket. On the other side of the grocery store was his favorite spot. A fresh bakery and sandwich counter.

Looking at all the deli meats and sandwich options was tough. Sandwiches were well out of his means. But! There were fresh snowflake rolls for $0.59 a piece. Calculating the math, he could get one Slim Jim, two rolls, and an apple. He would fill his water bottle in the sink, and it would be heavenly to eat on the bench, looking at flowers, and feeling like he accomplished so much in one morning.

The rest of the day was spent enjoying some time at the library, watching a movie on his phone with the Wi-Fi and making a comfortable nest on one of the couches. He was also able to download an extra movie for the rest of the weekend. Structure. The weather was damp, but warm enough. I was safe today.

Sunday was more of the same—walking, being involved with the town, convincing myself I was going to be ok. Except this time, there was a nagging feeling I couldn't shake. A tightness in my chest. The sense that I was in trouble, that everything I was doing was wrong. Not illegal—just wrong. Like I was a bad kid who'd wandered too far from the expectations, and from where I was supposed to be.

So far, I had been taking care of myself well enough this September, and sometimes I was better than ok - I was going to get through the school year, then the next year, then graduate, and leave for college and never look back. I knew that, even if I didn't have the courage to say it. I could see a future for me, with my own family, in my own world, and in a house without monsters.

I managed to shower at the town rec center, Mahoney, the kind of place no one really used anymore. I washed the clothes I wore yesterday in the sink and hung them to dry for a bit in the bathroom, hoping no one would notice. Standing there under flickering lights, I felt exposed, like I was doing something I wasn't allowed to do, even though no one had told me I couldn't.

The rec center itself felt like a relic: outdated bathrooms, echoing basketball courts, the smell of musty shoes and damp tile. It was never busy, which made it feel safer and lonelier at the same time. The only problem was distance. It was farther from Case Mountain than I wanted to walk, but it had walls. A lost-and-found box was in the corner, which was a place to find things and a place where people could walk in and just be.

The nagging feeling followed me when I left, showered as best as I could manage, and hungry. I have been hungry before, and this day, because of the strange anxiety, it was ok to have an empty stomach. In spite of my angst, it was a beautiful day in Manchester. I wound through Main Street, up Summit Street, past Buckley. Somewhere along the way, the air shifted. It got colder fast, as if I'd stepped into someone else's shadow. I shivered and pulled my hoodie tighter around my neck.

That's when the silver pickup appeared.

It came up fast behind me, the engine loud and sudden, and then it stopped, hard, about fifty feet ahead. Too close to the sidewalk. I flinched. My stomach dropped. Every part of me froze. I wanted to disappear, to be smaller. I remember thinking, 'This is it.' The monsters found me.....

For a split second, I was sure someone was going to get out of the truck. And waiting to see what could happen felt like a lifetime. What should I do? Yell. go willing, kick, scream? I didn't want to do something I couldn't undo. I just wish my body wasn't paralyzed and that my heart would stop trying to leave my chest.

A thin line of smoke swirled out the driver's side window, and just as suddenly as it had appeared, the truck peeled out, tires screaming as it sped away. It was as if I cared much more about the truck being on the road, than the truck cared about it startled me. The air changed back into a lovely day, just like nothing had happened, and I had to question, "Did something happen just to me?" What I didn't know then, what I couldn't name, was that the fear wasn't just about the truck. It was about loneliness, that this was an act of abandonment - and I was shown that I no longer mattered.

Chapter 7

Steven Ran

The last week of September was hard, but happy. Steven attended clubs like FACTS, the debate team, Dungeons and Dragons, and cross-country every day after school. Teachers, coaches, and staff were all pretty happy when they saw him. He felt great, like he was doing it, like he belonged. Although the weather was a bit cooler than he wanted, the month of September was moving on, and he was still content. He felt alive. By Friday, Steven was exhausted and waited until dark to set up his makeshift tent and go to sleep. The monsters he usually saw when he closed his eyes were not there. Instead, he woke up startled that he was still outside and on his own at dawn, fully rested.

This weekend was different. He would not have to worry about structure and finding places in town to get his needs met. There would be a bus to take him to the next cross-country meet. He was not going to be left out, with a faint excuse of family. He looked forward to going out of town, being with the team and wearing his royal blue running sneakers. This was the first out-of-town meet he could make, because it didn't require a ride across town.

The regional event was at UCONN, a large university hosting all eastern Connecticut high schools for the whole day. There were crowds and volunteers of all ages and each with different reasons to be there; moms with long puffy coats and piping, hot coffees, dads with beat up jeans and thick sweatshirts, crowds of teams with matching worn jerseys, knee socks (you could almost guess the smells looking at them). One mom brought doughnuts in flat boxes of all different colors with chocolate and frosting that stuck to the lid. Steven wanted to lick the sprinkles up off every ounce of the box, but instead delicately took the largest he could see. Breakfast was needed. He had saved a banana from the cafeteria yesterday, but the carbohydrates made him feel awake! Between the sugar and vibes, he felt powered up for his run. He felt energized.

***

Whenever I stood with my team, surrounded by their mothers with folding chairs and snack bags and the nosy dads with clipboards and booming voices,I kept my head down. I never knew if monsters existed only in the worlds I escaped from, or if everyone carried their own versions tucked behind practiced smiles. Maybe we all kept secrets. Or maybe I was the only one and sometimes felt like I couldn't hide mine.

I wanted so badly to talk to the other kids, to ask if they ever felt alone even when they were crowded in by family. I imagined telling someone that I could take care of myself, that I knew how to do things on my own and survive. But how could I know who was like me? How do you choose who to trust when your secrets feel like scars? I am not as likable as people think I am. My shame made the decisions for me.

"Oh, my God! Look at your arms!" a mother gasped, the one with the doughnuts and the too-wide smile. Before I could react, she lunged toward my wrist. I flinched back instinctively, her touch searing me like hot lava. Every nerve in my body lit up, my senses exploding in panic. I hadn't looked at myself for a long time, and hadn't realized the scrapes and bruises. Bug bites and cuts were part of the downside of living on my own. I felt strong on the inside, but I had not looked in a mirror for a longtime. When I thought of that, the memory of the microwave reflection made me shudder.

She pulled her hand back, laughing it off. "You must have sensitive skin! I've got medicine in the car, Benadryl or something.

You should take one after your races, sweetheart. It'll calm that right down."

What she saw and what I felt were two very different things. I had not realized the poison ivy rash, small cuts, and bruises had taken over my limbs, and people could see it as damage and pain. She said she could give me help, aid, like she was offering one of her doughnuts, not realizing she'd just scraped across a scabbed wound that I never let anyone touch. She wanted to show me love and kindness, yet without having any idea how to react or accept it, I just avoided eye contact. My fear of monsters was inside my mind, stitched into me along with my view of the world of adults.

Suddenly, Coach came and rounded us up. "Like herding cats…" he jovially muttered and seemed quite proud of himself as the group of us strutted to the blue tape between two large trees. There was every color of jersey you could think of, and the same went for all the runners. We all were in every shape and size, but we all had the same singular goal: run. Run to beat your score. Run your best. Run to help the team qualify. Run to give honor to your school. But for me, it felt like I was running for freedom. I imagined running and never stopping; just running until there was nothing left of me, my soul released. The line-up of the boys was crowded. Energy buzzed thick. The gun went off. My mind broke free. I ran.

I was in a pack for the first moments. I was normal! Then all my internal thoughts shut off. There was no fear, no monsters, and no one could touch me. Just my body working, this was as close to flying as I had ever been. I felt the ground kiss my feet, the grass embrace my power. I have learned to know only that I can perform through hunger, rashes, old shoes, and alone. This morning, I had none of those things. I was in the world, instead of a world apart. I just ran.

I do not know my time or place in the races. I just know I ran three races that morning. The spaces in between the races were also special. The campus is beautifully landscaped with old trees and gardens. Buildings that felt like large magic castles with all sorts of characters inhabiting them. For a brief second, I caught myself planning on how to live here, which tree could I sleep next to, and where I would hide my boulder. I snapped out of it, realizing that the world I had created could never exist anywhere outside of Case Mountain.

After a long morning that led into early afternoon, with more doughnuts, water bottles, and orange slices, the team all piled into the bus. Everyone was happy, exhausted, and successful. The bus felt warm with the vinyl seats and cozy, The seats were the softest I have been on in a while. The trip was not long, about 30 minutes, but I have no idea when we got back because I was gently woken by the boy next to me. The run, medicine, being surrounded by people, safety, and food in my stomach made the sleep so deep, dark, and satisfying. The day was good. Nightfall was welcomed, and I was calm.

Sunday morning was bright and different. I could almost feel the earth switch to a new hue or filter. I am not sure how to describe the energy, just that I felt brand new. After yesterday, I saw that new ideas and environments were possible.

On my way down Case, I saw some of my favorite people happily waving at me. Coach and Chunky were walking around outside, and their smiles always made me feel special. I jogged over to them to say good morning and spend time with Chunky if I could.

My clothes from yesterday were in my backpack, and I only had some dirty clothes for today. I had to ration my clean clothes for school tomorrow, and my only t-shirt was damp from washing it on Friday after school. These were the thoughts that filled my mind when I wasn't running or working in school. Careful calculations, escape plans, and worse case scenarios were always being monitored in my head. Sometimes, it got a bit quieter when I was busy, but it never went away.

Chunky's tail swished and swayed, and her gentle way of putting her head in my hands made me feel grounded. All the other noise in my head could finally quiet down. Her fur was warm and smelled faintly of coffee and sunshine, and for a moment, the damp shirt, the rationed clothes, the constant calculations of what I needed to get through this next week slipped away. Chunky didn't care about any of that. She just stood there, solid and patient, reminding me that there were places where I didn't have to be perfect—only present.

Coach looked down on us both with kindness. He never mentioned my dirty clothes or the fact that he saw me every morning coming out of Case. I knew he watched for me. Sometimes I was glad to have someone know I made it to another day. Other times, the shame, fear, and secrets were hard to leave unspoken. Yet they were.

Chapter 8

Coach

On Case Mountain, where the road is old and narrow and only one lane by the waterfall, two women met head-on. With two opposing stop signs there was no space for bodies or cars to pass without someone choosing to wait for the other to go first.

One afternoon, I watched the worst of humanity come to the narrow road. One woman was in her old station wagon, drunk, lipstick smeared onto her teeth like a careless confession, and her mall-era hairdo stiff with defiance. She refused to back up, refused to yield. The other driver was a woman in a blue SUV, of approximately the same age and equally capable of reversing. She also refused to respond with reason and instead reacted in rage.

For women who might otherwise look like gentle grandmothers, something feral surfaced. Teeth bared. Voices snarled. Hands flung wildly into the air. What should have been a brief pause turned into a ten-minute standoff of venom and spectacle. Insults from the car windows were shouted, peace was destroyed, and the tiny waterfall lane felt violated.

Their words lashed out at everything nearby: dogs tugged at leashes, children played without context, men worried on the road above, and me, standing there, absorbed in it all. No one was spared. The mountain echoed with the sound of hatred.

There was Steven sitting blankly on the rocks watching the women curse, yell, and abuse each other from afar. They kept blowing their horns, and being mean for the sake of being right, or demanding to be first. I noticed Steven. He looked sickened and sad.

And in that moment, I understood something unsettling: how thin the façade of civility really is. We are taught that manners are owed only when it is convenient, when we are comfortable, when we are not asked to yield. Courtesy, it seems, is reserved for the deserving, not the desperate. But who decides who is needy? Was it the woman too proud to reverse? The one too intoxicated to reason? The children forced to witness adult ugliness? Or those of us who choose for ourselves a new path?

Watching Steven, wondering if this is how trauma is passed down—not always through violence done to us directly, but through violence we are made to witness. Anger we have to swallow, making the world feel like poison. Through moments when people forget they are being watched, the monsters' rage is louder than their restraint when supervised.

Steven broke his stare, and so did I. As soon as he decided to be free of this mess, he turned his body and head and saw his best friend, Chunky. He gave a wave like always from afar to us both. His face lit up at being acknowledged. Then he walked home away, from the street and into the woods.

I know I should not have made watching out for Steven my job. But every morning the dog and I waited to make sure Steven made it out, and we watched for him to return. We stood at the front of the yard in the rain and darkness. I couldn't help the nagging pull and my curiosity about Steven. Abby told me multiple times to mind my own business, that it was not my place. Yet, every morning, she would ask if I had spotted him. On Sunday, seeing him dragging out of the path to walk into town, he looked thin and haggard. Don't get me wrong. He was still a very handsome, happy boy, yet his eyes no longer looked bright. I was eager to get a better look at him, so Chunky and I waved him down. He glanced up, shrugged his body off the and walked past the road rage scene.

He interacted with people as if they were shadows, and he was in another world. His eyes did not shift, They stayed down on the ground, and he walked over with a half-jog like always.

"Well," I called over to him. "I could use your good knees to help me change the oil in my rider before I mow the lawn." Steven nodded as he rubbed his face into the dog's fur. "Wanna stay and help me around the house?"

Steven, as always, didn't say much, and he moved a bit slower than his normally energetic self. I opened the garage bay and set up a chair for him to sit on. I chatted nonstop with Steven as I was always relieved to see him safe and sound.

This Sunday, I'd woken up, and it had felt different, like there was pressure in the air and the neighborhood was a balloon. I kept pushing the anxiety away, tried to get my chores done and enjoy the morning. Sometimes, when I missed my son, Steven helped me feel not so lonely. I was grateful.

I dabbled and tinkered, while explaining to Steven this and that. We both lost track of time. Righty tighty, lefty loosey. He absorbed everything as if I were an alien describing a brand-new Earth. Quiet, wide-eyed, so eager. I noticed he had a smudge of grease on his shirt. "You might want to wash that right away, so it doesn't stain."

I felt instantly bad. I could see shame and panic cross Steven's face, and I felt like I had embarrassed him. "Maybe I can ask Abby to throw that shirt in for a quick rinse. Here let me," as I reached over to help him take the shirt off. Steven jumped in the air and let out a squeak. He was not used to being touched, and a man's hand felt so different from the mother's hand who'd grabbed him yesterday at the meet.

"Oh ok…settle down. Would you like me to help you wash the grease off?"

Steven stood paralyzed.

"Tell you what, I have an old work shirt hanging in the laundry room drying rack, why don't you go inside the house, put that on, and help yourself to the washer. I will be here trying to drain the oil, and we will just keep working. And, if your clothes aren't done in an hour, you can stay and have lasagne for dinner with Abby and me."

Steven nodded, and his eyes returned to their normal, happy setting. He got up, swallowed, picked up his backpack, and, with his head down, walked like a robot into the house. Chunky followed him, her tail wagging and ears high, as if she was on the lookout for any danger.

When Steven looked down at the stain, he looked horrified. There was no way that would wash off in the sink. This shirt is now done, and the calculations began… If I can dry the shirt at the campsite and maybe stop and use the hand dryer at Cumberland Farms for my track uniform, that would get me through until Tuesday. I would have to find another shirt to replace this one. That would make four shirts in total. Now that the weather is getting cooler, sweatpants would have to be found…

Coach didn't understand why Steven was slow to move and process a simple grease stain, but it made him feel like he should finally question the kid about what was going on. Why was he living on Case Mountain?

Steven walked past Abby and blushed.

I shouted to Abby, "I told Steven to use our washer to remove some grease!" in hopes that any embarrassment would disappear. Loneliness hits everyone differently. I never expected to be so alone after my son moved, my friends got "stuck in their ways," and people moved on, or away. I often think I can't afford to lose another when someone passes. I didn't mean to overwhelm Steven who although he was a bright boy, looked more ragged than ever. I probably should have not chatted all day. I knew my loneliness was not one of his problems.

When the oil finished draining, I squatted down beside him and pointed to the drain pan. "Pull that out, and we'll have to put the lug nut back before adding oil."

Steven crouched carefully onto the garage floor and reached under the mower. Slowly, gingerly, he pulled the full pan out. I thought about telling him it wasn't such a big deal, that he didn't need to be so careful—but I didn't want him to think there was anything wrong with how he was being so careful. I knew he wanted to help me.

As he stood, balancing the pan between his two hands, our eyes met. Steven gasped, and as if in slow motion, the oil pan slipped from his hands. It hit the floor with a bomb-like effect, warm oil splashing across us and the mower. With my glasses getting splattered, I stumbled back. I froze for a moment, startled and shaken. I was used to messes when working on my machines.

But Steven…

The crash of metal on concrete must have felt like a gunshot. He dropped into himself instantly, as if expecting to die. And then he grasped his head, and a flashback gripped him. He lost his gravity.

***

He was eleven again, standing in front of the refrigerator. His mother was sick on the couch, a damp cloth on her forehead, asking for soup. A heavy bowl of soup had been brought over by a nice neighbor and put on the top shelf. When he went to get it, it slipped through his fingers, just like the oil pan. The lid had been loose. The contents hit the floor with force and spraying everywhere, splattering cabinets and shelves in a sudden explosion of minestrone.

His mother screamed; shrill, furious, unforgettable, cutting right through him. He had tried for years to erase the memory, but it still returned in jagged fragments, flashing like broken film.

***

Now, in the garage, he could not look at me.

"Steven! Steven! Hey, are you okay? Are you hurt?" But he was already curled into a fetal position, eyes clenched so tight I wasn't sure if oil had splashed in them or if he was simply locked inside to his own horror.

I reached out and touched him. His reaction was indescribable; visceral, wild, almost feral. He twitched, whimpered, sobbing without words or sounds.

So I didn't move. I just laid my oily hands on him, steady and still, letting their weight speak for me. Letting them tell him he wasn't alone. Trying to steady him and help him with any injuries. It seemed like what was hurt was more mentally inside than on the outside.

Abby came running out into the garage with pasta sauce splattered on her shirt. "What happened!?!" She reached over and grabbed my eyeglasses off my face, and in one fluid motion, wiped them on her shirt while getting to the floor to cradle Steven in her arms. Swiftly, and I don't know how, she moved him to the porch.

"Clean this up and I will help him!" she ordered, and the control of the situation was no longer my issue. She knew exactly what to do while I stood there, still frozen.

As I went to the back of the garage to grab a random bag of kitty litter, I heard the sun porch door slam and the familiar pounding footsteps of a runner. I knew Steven would run before I could yell out. I tried to run after him, but he was too fast. I turned, and we stared at each other. Silence fell on the house. We moved through cleaning up the mess like zombies as if we were moving through wet sand. The sound of my heart throbbed in my head as I was so worried about Steven.

We sat at the kitchen table, sipping tea, not wanting to say anything as the hours slipped away. Even Chunky didn't want to go to bed.

"That's it! Abby. Get your boots and flashlight. We are going to get him." I grabbed the leash for Chunky. She was just as worried as both of us. We cannot leave him out there."

We were determined to find him and walked up to Case Mountain, and the sound of the lovely waterfall was gentle. As the night set in, the mountain was getting darker and more difficult to search.

"STEVEN!"

We called and called, following the trail up the hill. There was no sign of anyone left in the woods. This place was usually busy, being one of the most photographed hiking spots in all of Connecticut, always full of dogs and people. But as the night crept in, it transformed. The laughter faded, the paths emptied, and the mountain became a desolate place.

After hiking to the top and searching everywhere, Chunky started to whine, and I was too tired to go on. Abby grabbed my hand and, with her strength, pulled me back onto the path toward home.

Halfway down the hill, I thought I heard twigs snap. I thought I saw something to the left of us in the thick brush. We paused, called out, and flashed our light, but the woods only stared back at us, colorful and yet barren, with no Steven.

This wasn't what I had pictured for him. Somehow, I'd imagined he was just fine, and always safe, living in some magical place. I knew he did not go "home," and I wasn't sure why. But seeing the mountain for what it truly was made me even sadder. No child should be here like this.

As we walked home in silence, neither of us knew quite what to do. At this point, I knew we needed to report him missing to the police, but the thought was hard to say out loud. I was sure Abby would make the call once we got home, and I wouldn't have to. She was that kind of person, someone who never hesitated to do the right thing. She lived her life with quiet dignity, never needing to explain herself or show off.

Rounding the lawn, Chunky leaped forward. I let her off the leash once we were back in our front lawn, and she bolted toward the front porch, nuzzling a heap that was huddled there.

As we came closer, the sight etched itself into my mind. It was Steven, covered in splattered oil, mud, and curled up as the neglected child that he really was. We had all watched him being neglected. The whole town must have questioned it, yet, out of fear of getting involved or of learning the truth that might be too hard to hear, we pretended as much as Steven did. The only clean part of him now was the tear tracks running down his face.

Abby bent down, met him at eye level, and wrapped her arms around him in a way only a mother could. He sobbed, and she held him tight. I once again was frozen. I am not sure if it was fear that I'd hurt him, or that someone else had.

I quickly got the dog inside and opened the door so Abby could help Steven in. Somehow, we all knew, without saying a word, that we were in this together. Whatever trouble Steven was in, it was our trouble now, too.

Chapter 9

Abby

I had held my fears for Steven deep in my chest for quite a while. As the Summer had progressed, I noticed him more and more. What nagged at me wasn't how pleasant he was to the dog and Coach, or how sweet he was to help us when we were outside. It was the moments when he thought no one was looking. His head was down, eyes were sunken, and his legs looked heavy.

As I now all but carried this man/child covered in oil and mud to the bathroom, I was struck by how much he surrendered to me. Steven always had a smile and seemed as if there was nothing he couldn't handle; yet, in this moment, all resemblance to that child was broken. There were no words we could exchange. We just moved together, leaning our body weight on each other through the space.

I set Steven up in the bathroom for a shower and asked him to call out to me if the engine oil wouldn't rinse off. "I could sprinkle baking soda on your hair and neck area if it doesn't rinse off," I offered. As I started bustling around him, my mother's intuition sprang to life once again, and I knew I was needed.

Steven responded with gulps and nods, but I was scared for him. Gone was the "eager to please" and wide eyed-boy, having been replaced by a hollow shell. Bruises, rashes, and cuts on skinny limbs that appeared to want to curl up and shield the rest of the body in a detached state were all that was there. He was more like a ghost, disconnected from a tortured body.

He kept his head down as I quietly moved out of his space. I could feel his energy. I searched the house, looking for pajamas for him and hoped to leave them before he put on his original clothes. I cracked open the door and peeked through the small opening. I noticed he had not moved from the center of the bathroom. I reached my arm through the crack and dropped the pajamas on the top of the sink. Then I slowly went to retreat.

As I was leaving, I wanted to warn him, "Steven, be careful with our hot water, sometimes it can turn really hot," but I accidentally got a glimpse of his secret. He had started lifting his shirt, and the scars on his back told a very different life than I had imagined. I thought that to create such a wonderful boy, he must have come from a happy, magical place. But, in that place, those scars would not be there on his back. Startled, I shut the door, leaving him, letting him keep his secrets.

Remembering his clothes were in the washing machine from earlier, I finished his laundry. It was an old practice to wash young men's clothes. All cotton and soft, much like these young men are, still innocent and vulnerable. Going into my son Joey's bedroom to set it up for Steven for the night felt strange. I can't tell if it felt good, sad, or just heavy, but I was most grateful to be able to make the bed I used to make all the time. I laid out an extra-fluffy blanket and a new pillow so I knew the bed would be perfect. I just wanted to make Steven feel….I don't know anymore…

When Steven came out of the bathroom, his face was red. Like he was scratched clean. The tear stains were gone, and so was the joy he usually displayed. The pajamas were huge on his frame, but Steven didn't seem to notice. Coach waited for him to sit down, and I immediately sprang into action, making him peppermint tea and warming up a plate of dinner. Steven took the hint to eat and attempted to lift his head. He was so worn out that lifting the fork looked hard, yet he scarfed all the food down. Coach and I just sat very still, stunned.

There were so many questions we wanted to ask him. "Is someone looking for you to come home?" "What happened?" "Do you want to stay the night?" I asked these questions as slowly and patiently as I could, although Inside my chest I felt enraged! I wanted to fight for this soul, keep him safe, and comfortable.

Chunky also sat ,waiting patiently for Steven to share.

All we got was head nods. No, no one was looking for him. No, he did not know who to tell he was here. Yes, he was willing to wait for the sunrise, and he muttered that he would go to school because he never missed a day.

He got up and laid down on the porch with Chunky after we were done at the table. He didn't want much else; just to lie on the porch with his only friend, which was the dog, was all he could do. He was asleep within seconds, not minutes, and I didn't wake him to bring him upstairs. Instead, I covered him with a thick flannel blanket and watched over him throughout the night.

In the early morning, while the sun was still rising, Steven lay very still, staring into the backyard. I tried not to bother him, even though I still had so many questions.

I whispered to Coach, "I think I know where his father works, out at the machine shop."

Coach whispered, "You should tell him we have Steven. They are probably worried sick."

Instead of discussing with the either of them, I took matters to the streets. I needed to think about how to help Steven.

Early morning is for my sneakers, when the "old school women" in the neighborhood, out of sheer boredom, put on their sneakers to walk in the early morning up and down Spring St. With out-of-date gym clothes and a windbreaker on, I met up with my two neighbors of the last thirty years. We can almost tell when we will meet at the corner and walk our 2.5 miles, with our sneakers, gossip, and water bottles that we switch hands every hundred meters. In the last thirty years, our butts have turned flat, our stomachs round, our hair is now dyed a weird off-color shade, and our eyes are crinkled in the corners. Yet, these women are my kindred spirits by sheer location and friendship through half my lifespan. We can solve almost any problem with our sneakers on, and this morning was no different. We devised a plan to call and report Steven to DCF, but first, we'd tell the school.

"They say time heals all wounds" (1974, Rose Kennedy), but it's not time. It's work, processing, perspective, and safety. I understood that the three of us, Coach, Steven and me, are going to have to work this out. I can no longer ignore Steven creeping out of the woods at dawn, like a frightened bunny, worried that someone would notice and grab him. I was going to call the school. Steven will get a ride to school from Coach, after we all eat a good breakfast. The smell of cinnamon, fresh honey, and oatmeal with coffee was just what we all needed. But none of us could talk. We all kept our heads down, no eye contact, and no whispering of basics.

After that first night and day, our lives forever changed, and we started working out our routine.. Piece by piece, Coach and I learned that Steven had run away from home. There was an open file with DCF for neglect, which was investigated three times in the last five years. Steven's case was closed and unsubstantiated. His mother, a week after Steven stayed with us, showed up at our driveway. She had not realized that he stayed after school everyday for clubs and sports, and so she came too early, and Steven was not home. I cannot say if that would have changed anything. I was not scared for Steven. My ability to care for him outweighed her ability to neglect him.

That night, we got Steven his own cell phone, so he could call his mother and father directly. I wanted him to start making his own choices, along with letting us know when he needed a ride or help. The odd thing was, he didn't know either parent's cell number. I had to call DCF for that info and keep it in case they were ever needed. Need and want are two very different things, and I believe Steven someday may want them.

As his acting mother, I watched Steven grow and accept a truth in life that I had always hoped he would find; that love does not hurt, courage can be quiet, and strength does not have to be strong to be real. I saw him learn that being a man does not require hardness or cruelty, or proving himself through putting others beneath him. Instead, he discovered that gentleness could be a form of courage, that nurturing others could coexist with being vulnerable. In his healing, I came to understand something too: that the greatest protection I could ever wish for him was not dominance over the world, but peace within himself, something no one could ever take away.

Chapter 10

What happened next:

The school year progressed. When Fall sports ended, Steven continued with track. When school was off, Steven would sleep. Sometimes up to 16 hours a day. We understood. This was his way of grieving, resting, and healing. Spending a month on his own in the woods left unseen scars, and living with monsters left real physical marks that would never go away.

The holidays were calm and peaceful. Our son brought his family to our house for Christmas, and it was the most Steven had ever been around that many people. There were some hard moments, and other wonderful ones, but Steven blossomed with rest after the holidays. By spring, he had grown four inches and was tanned, muscular, and as handsome as ever, but he never cared about any of that. He always seemed to judge each and every person with a keen eye.

We never pressured Steven. He stayed very quiet. Chunky stayed by his side. The unanswered questions that at first hung in the air grew into respectful inclusiveness and acceptance.

In the Summer, Steven worked with the Parks and Rec department as a Junior Park Maintenance Worker. Working outside suited him, with his solid frame, scruffy chin, and light laugh.

One day in July, digging around the trees to install watering systems with a small crew at Mahoney, his buddy came by with some water. Steven stood up, "Thanks, man…"

Steven glanced up to see a silver truck in the distance, lingering by the stop sign. The tinted windows were cracked open, releasing a thin stream of cigarette smoke. Although startled, Steven, unlike before when he'd encountered the truck last year, he did not flinch but stared back.

There are no monsters or heroes in this world, the way we imagine them when we are young. There are only people; people carrying fragments of themselves they have never learned how to hold. Some try to piece themselves together with love, care, and gratitude. Others choose judgment. Some cling to the convention of victims and losers, because those roles ask less of them than accountability ever would.

What matters is not what you survived, but what you chose to become after surviving it.

Steven went on to States with his cross-country team in his Junior and Senior years. He was a respectful house guest and found his voice. He did

Chunky passed away in the Fall after Steven's high school graduation, and he'd left for college. We cremated her and have her ashes on the porch. We fight every day about getting a puppy. Steven and Joey already had one picked out for Labor Day vacation….

Heather Plourde

Broken Bits

I only trust the broken bits
That have been shattered and thrown
Across the floor
Picked up and mended, impacted but true
Finding their place to whole and new

The glassy surface I can't buy
Their appearance of perfection and
Never knowing whats inside
Their reflection as trustworthy as it seems

Instead I focus on the strength, wisdom
And search to repair
The beauty of not disguising what's more
Underneath, as we become aware

For broken bits demonstrate
A person worthy,
That passed many test
That decided they were worthy
And their bonds of all their pieces best

Afterword

This book is a work of fiction, although it is deeply influenced by my experiences working in the mental health field. Over the years, I have witnessed many stories of resilience, struggle, trauma, unrest, survival, and healing. The human experience is unavoidable. No matter who we are, we all spend our lives trying to understand ourselves while learning how to endure pain, connection, and loss.

In this story, each character carries the same wounds in different forms. Each one struggles with loneliness and wrestles with their life. Each character is surviving something invisible to the outside world and faces moral conflict, grief, fear, or loss, and longing. Though their struggles look different, their needs are remarkably similar: safety, understanding, belonging, and hope.

Grief is one of the few universal experiences that still feels entirely personal. Every person born into this world will eventually lose someone or something they love, and not always by death, sometimes by choice. Yet, grief always arrives inside our chest ,as if no one else could possibly understand it. It is unsolvable in many ways. There is no cure for it, no perfect stage to complete, and no final answer that makes it disappear. We simply learn how to carry it.

Questions about existence are equally universal. Clients of every age ask some version of the same question: Why am I here? Why me? The search for meaning follows us throughout life.

Some people discover purpose in relationships, some in work, some in survival itself. Others spend years searching without a landing. That uncertainty can be frightening, but it is also profoundly necessary for an impactful life.

Longing may be one of the most defining traits of humanity. We ache to be loved, wanted, needed, and understood. We want connection, yet we fear rejection. Many people struggle with the painful question of why they cannot connect with everyone around them. The answer is rarely simple. Human beings are complicated, shaped by fear, memory, attachment, and survival. Perhaps that is the point of the story. We are all more alike than we realize.

As I wrote these characters, I often found myself asking which one I would most want to counsel. Surprisingly, the answer is not always the one in the greatest crisis.

Steven Cookies is the character I would struggle with the most as a clinician. Not because he is beyond help, but because he is not ready for it. Steven has had opportunities to ask for support. He could have told a teacher, a coach, an office staff member, or another trusted adult about what was happening to him. Yet he remained on his own. Silence, however, is often its own survival strategy.

A therapist meeting Steven too early would likely focus immediately on his biological parents and childhood trauma. But with some individuals, especially those with ASD or significant trauma histories, pushing too quickly can intensify symptoms rather than relieve them. There is truth in the old saying that therapy can sometimes make things feel worse before they feel better. Steven does not need pressure. He needs time and space.

Before Steven could truly engage in therapy, he would need stability, patience, kindness, and time. He would need the opportunity to form healthy attachments and experience consistency before revisiting neglect and abandonment.

When Steven was finally ready, therapy would not begin with uncovering every painful memory. It would begin with the present: addressing the behavior patterns and fears shaped by his childhood, his fear of sleep, fear of being seen as a problem, his hyper-vigilance, his difficulty trusting others. Healing would come slowly through direction, goals, structure, compassion, and connection.

In many ways, Steven represents something seen often in real life: people who survive by enduring quietly. People who are not refusing help because they are difficult, but because survival taught them silence was safer.

If this story leaves readers with anything, I hope it is compassion — for others, and for themselves. Every person carries a story that has shaped them. Some wounds are visible. Many are not. But beneath the surface, most people are simply trying to survive, connect, and be understood.

Why This Story Matters

Writing about acute stress disorder and mental health is important because many individuals, especially adolescents, experience intense emotional challenges that often go unseen or misunderstood. Conditions like Acute Stress Disorder can develop rapidly after trauma, yet they are frequently overlooked, minimized, or misidentified.

Through storytelling, this book aims to shed light on the internal experiences behind outward appearances, particularly in young people who may seem "fine" on the surface. By exploring these themes in a realistic and human way, Heather hopes to reduce stigma, encourage early recognition of symptoms, and foster more compassionate conversations about mental health.

Ultimately, this work is not just about one character's journey—it is about creating awareness, validating lived experiences, and reminding readers that mental health struggles deserve attention, understanding, and care.

About the Author

Heather Plourde, LPC, is a licensed professional counselor with a background in psychology and anthropology, bringing a unique, research-informed perspective to her writing. With years of experience working in clinical settings, including high-acuity behavioral health environments and community-based programs, she has dedicated her career to understanding human behavior, trauma, and resilience.

In addition to her clinical work, Heather has successfully developed and led programs focused on mental health awareness, public education, and accessible care. Her passion for storytelling stems from a desire to bridge the gap between clinical knowledge and real-life experience—making complex emotional struggles more visible, relatable, and understood.

www.ingramcontent.com/pod-product-compliance
Lightning Source LLC
LaVergne TN
LVHW051044210926
848486LV00001B/9
* 9 7 8 1 9 6 0 5 9 6 9 8 7 *